WIDGET & THE PUPPY

Lyn Rossiter McFarland   Pictures by Jim McFarland

Farrar Straus Giroux · New York

To Laddie and Chili, Bonnie and Shane,
our Newfie friends

Text copyright © 2004 by Lyn Rossiter McFarland
Illustrations copyright © 2004 by Jim McFarland
All rights reserved
Distributed in Canada by Douglas & McIntyre Ltd.
Color separations by Prime Digital Media
Printed and bound in the United States of America by Phoenix Color Corporation
Designed by Jay Colvin
First edition, 2004
1 3 5 7 9 10 8 6 4 2

www.fsgkidsbooks.com

Library of Congress Cataloging-in-Publication Data
McFarland, Lyn Rossiter.
   Widget and the puppy / Lyn Rossiter McFarland ; pictures by Jim McFarland.— 1st ed.
      p. cm.
   Summary: When a stray puppy shows up, Widget the dog receives no help from
the cats as he tries to look after it.
   ISBN 0-374-38429-0
   [1. Dogs—Fiction. 2. Cats—Fiction.] I. McFarland, Jim, 1935– ill. II. Title.

PZ7.M4784614Wl 2004
[E]—dc21

2002044671

Widget lived in a little house with Mrs. Diggs and the girls.
One day a stranger came to the door.

"Look," said Mrs. Diggs. "We have a visitor."

Widget looked. The girls looked.
It was a puppy. A *big* puppy.
"Widget, you watch the puppy," said Mrs. Diggs,
"while I go find his owner."

Widget watched the puppy.

He watched the puppy eat his food.

He watched the puppy eat the girls' food.

He watched the puppy
take a drink and
slobber water
all over the floor.

He watched the puppy drool
and roll around on everyone's bed.

The girls watched Widget watching the puppy.
They thought Widget was a terrible puppy-watcher.

The girls tried to sneak out the door. The puppy saw them.

The puppy followed the girls.
Widget followed the puppy.

The puppy wanted to play a game with the girls.
He played Chase the Girls around the Yard and up a Tree.

The girls hissed at the puppy.

They growled at Widget.
It wasn't their job to watch the puppy.
It wasn't their job to play with him, either.

Widget watched the puppy find other games to play.
He watched the puppy play Chase the Frogs out of the Pond.

He watched the puppy play
Find the Treasure in the Trash.

He watched the puppy play
Chew Up All the Toys.

Widget even watched the puppy play Catch Widget's Tail.
Puppy-watching was hard work.
Widget could hardly keep his eyes open.

Oh no! Widget had fallen asleep. The puppy! He'd lost the puppy! What would Mrs. Diggs say? Widget was in big trouble.

He ran around the yard.
He saw the girls. They were looking at something.

Widget looked where the girls were looking.
He saw the puppy's tail.

It wasn't wagging! The puppy was stuck
in the groundhog's hole.
He needed to be rescued.

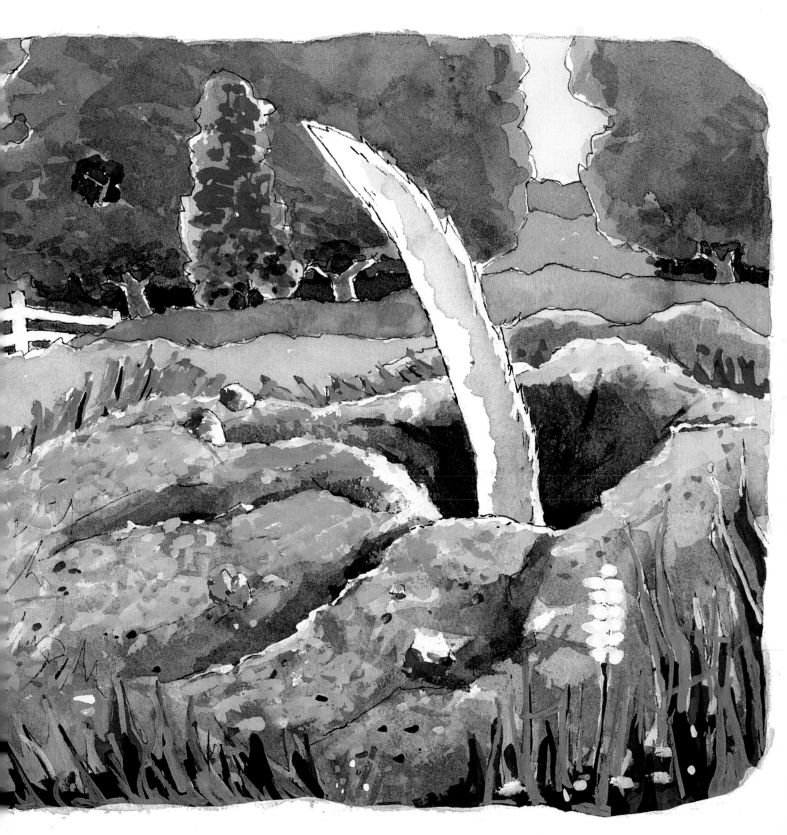

Widget dug down until he reached the puppy's nose.
The puppy was happy to see Widget.
He gave Widget a big, sloppy kiss.
Widget dug the puppy out.

Now Widget wanted to play. The puppy did, too.
They played Widget's favorite game,
Digging Up the Woodchuck's Hole.
They had lots of fun.

"Widget!" called Mrs. Diggs.
"Look who's here."
It was the puppy's owner.

Widget and the puppy played
Catch the *Puppy's* Tail
all the way back to the house.

Widget and the puppy got a bath.

The girls did, too.
It was time for the puppy to leave.

Mrs. Diggs gave Widget a pat.
"Widget was a wonderful
puppy-watcher," she said.
"Right, girls?"